10/13

26 MAR 2018

KU-181-304

STREAM

WOLFHOLD

STEVE BARLOW AND STEVE SKIDMORE
Illustrated by ANDREW CHIU

SOUTHWARK LIBRARIES
SK 2371276 7

TITLES AT THIS LEVEL

Fiction

978 1 4451 1314 2 pb

978 1 4451 1316 6 pb

978 1 4451 1318 0 pb

978 1 4451 1815 4 pb

978 1 4451 1814 7 pb

978 1 4451 1816 1 pb

Graphic fiction

978 1 4451 1322 7 pb

978 1 4451 1320 3 pb

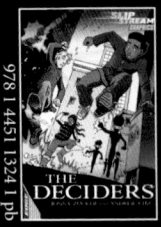

978 1 4451 1324 1 pb

978 1 4451 1803 1 pb

978 1 4451 1802 4 pb

978 1 4451 1804 8 pb

Non-fiction

978 1 4451 1358 6 pb

978 1 4451 1360 9 pb

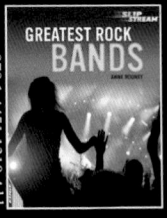

978 1 4451 1310 4 hb
978 1 4451 1359 3 pb

978 1 4451 1956 4 hb

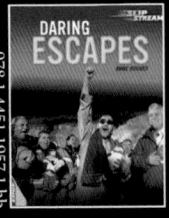

978 1 4451 1957 1 hb

978 1 4451 1955 7 hb

SLIP STREAM

WOLFHOLD

STEVE BARLOW AND STEVE SKIDMORE
Illustrated by ANDREW CHIU

EDGE
FRANKLIN WATTS
LONDON•SYDNEY

London Borough
of Southwark

B

SK 2371276 7

Askews & Holts	18-Oct-2013
JF	£5.99 ✓

First published in 2013 by
Franklin Watts
338 Euston Road
London NW1 3BH

Franklin Watts Australia
Level 17/207 Kent Street
Sydney NSW 2000

Text © Steve Barlow and Steve Skidmore 2013
Illustration © Franklin Watts 2013

The rights of Steve Barlow and Steve Skidmore to be identified as the authors of this Work have been asserted in accordance with the Copyright, Designs and Patents Act, 1988.

All rights reserved

A CIP catalogue record for this book is available from the British Library.

(ebook) ISBN: 978 1 4451 1820 8
(pb) ISBN: 978 1 4451 1814 7
(library ebook) ISBN: 978 1 4451 2606 7

Series Editors: Adrian Cole and Jackie Hamley
Series Advisors: Diana Bentley and Dee Reid
Series Designer: Peter Scoulding

1 3 5 7 9 10 8 6 4 2

Printed in China

Franklin Watts is a division of
Hachette Children's Books,
an Hachette UK company.
www.hachette.co.uk

CONTENTS

Chapter 1	A Strange Place	6
Chapter 2	A Strange Village	10
Chapter 3	No Way Out	14
Chapter 4	The Villagers	22

CHAPTER 1

A STRANGE PLACE

Tom woke up.

He was a strange bed...

...in a strange room...

...in a strange house.

Tom lived in London...

...but he was not in London now!

Tom ran out of the house.

He saw a girl.

"I'm Megan," she said.

"Do you know why you are here?"

"I don't know," said Tom. "I think there was a fight but I can't remember."

THE BLEEDING LAMB
THE BLEEDING LAMB
OLFHOLE

CHAPTER 2

A STRANGE VILLAGE

Tom went into the shop.

He tried to buy a newspaper.

The shopkeeper shook his head.

"No papers in Wolfhold."

"Can I make a call or use the internet?" asked Tom.

"No phones or computers here," said the man.

OPEN

"I want to go home," said Tom.

"Is there a bus out of here?"

"No bus," said Megan.

"What about a taxi?" asked Tom.

"No taxis," said Megan. "There's no way out of Wolfhold."

OPEN

CHAPTER 3

NO WAY OUT

Tom set off across the moor.

"There's no way out," called Megan.

But Tom kept going.

The road came to an end.

But Tom kept going.

Tom walked past a huge rock.

There were rabbits on the moor.

There were deer and goats.

But there were no roads,

and no people.

Tom came to a high fence.

He touched it.

"Aaargh!!"

He got a shock.

Then Megan was beside him.

"This is just the first fence. There are at least three more. No one has got past three."

"Come back to the village," said Megan.

Tom shook his head. "Why am I here?" he shouted.

"If only I could remember!"

CHAPTER 4

THE VILLAGERS

Tom followed Megan down the hill.

It was getting dark.

The moon was full.

They came to the huge rock.

The people of the village were

coming towards them.

"Soon you will understand," said Megan.

The villagers began to change.

Tom was scared.

"We have to get out of here!" he cried.

"Those people are werewolves!"

"I know," said Megan. "Welcome to the pack."

Then Tom remembered.

And he understood.

Wolfhold was the prison for his kind.

He would never leave Wolfhold.

SLIP STREAM

WHITE WATER WIPE OUT!

ROGER HURN

EDGE

Rick and Ali are on a school trip.
They go white water rafting and it is brilliant!

Then Rick decides to try the out-of-bounds Hell Hole.
Will Ali be able to save his friend?

SLIP STREAM
ROBBED!
ANNE CASSIDY
CASH POINT
EDGE

Tommy is late and his sister Lizzie is worried. She is told that Big Alex is taking him to the cash machine.

Lizzie is sure that Tommy is about to be robbed. What can she do?

FOR TEACHERS

About SLIPSTREAM

Slipstream is a series of expertly levelled books designed for pupils who are struggling with reading. Its unique three-strand approach through fiction, graphic fiction and non-fiction gives pupils a rich reading experience that will accelerate their progress and close the reading gap.

At the heart of every Slipstream fiction book is a great story. Easily accessible words and phrases ensure that pupils both decode and comprehend, and the high interest stories really engage older struggling readers.

Whether you're using Slipstream Level 1 for Guided Reading or as an independent read, here are some suggestions:

1. Make each reading session successful. Talk about the text before the pupil starts reading. Introduce any unfamiliar vocabulary.

2. Encourage the pupil to talk about the book using a range of open questions. For example, how else could the story end?

3. Discuss the differences between reading fiction, graphic fiction and non-fiction. What do they prefer?

Slipstream Level 1 photocopiable **WORKBOOK**
ISBN: 978 1 4451 1798 0
available – download free sample worksheets from:
www.franklinwatts.co.uk

For guidance, SLIPSTREAM Level 1 – Wolfhold has been approximately measured to:

National Curriculum Level: 2c
Reading Age: 7.0–7.6
Book Band: Turquoise

ATOS: 1.5*
Guided Reading Level: H
Lexile® Measure (confirmed): 110L

***Please check actual Accelerated Reader™ book level and quiz availability at www.arbookfind.co.uk**